Chili-Chili-Chin-Chin

BELLE YANG

SILVER WHISTLE ❀ HARCOURT BRACE & COMPANY

San Diego   New York   London   ❀   Printed in Singapore

Chili-Chili-Chin-Chin, a furry little donkey I am.

When I run, my bells sing "chili-chili-chin-chin."

That's how I got my name.

Some people say, "Chili-Chili-Chin-Chin,
you sweet donkey, I want to ride you.

I want to own you."

"Oh, no, never! Impossible!" I tell them,
and send them on their way.

"Chili-chili-chin-chin."

I'm not a cow.

I'm not a horse.

I'm not a puppy on a leash.

No, not me.

Chili-Chili-Chin-Chin I am.

No one can catch me . . .

except the boy who gave me my name.

"Chili-chili-chin-chin."

I take him in spring

to find blossoms,

in summer

to watch turtles swim,

in autumn

to pick persimmons,

and in winter to make fresh tracks.

"Chili-chili-chin-chin."

He sings me lullabies.

He's my friend.

I am his.

He gives me room to be alone with my thoughts.

He knows my dreams whether I say anything or not.

I'd take him anywhere.

When we are together I can be me.

"Chili-chili-chin-chin. Chili-chili-chin-chin."

Chili-Chili-Chin-Chin I am.

Library of Congress Cataloging-in-Publication Data
Yang, Belle.
Chili-Chili-Chin-Chin/Belle Yang.—1st ed.
p.   cm.
"Silver Whistle."
Summary: Chili-Chili-Chin-Chin, a free-spirited donkey,
tells of his love for the boy who named him after the sound his bells make.
ISBN 0-15-202006-3
[1. Donkeys—Fiction.]   I. Title.
PZ7.Y1925Ch   1999
[E]—dc21   98-15891

First edition
A C E F D B

The illustrations in this book were done in gouache on watercolor paper.
The display type was set in Rio Medio.
The text type was set in Spectrum Semibold.
Color separations by Tien Wah Press, Singapore
Printed and bound by Tien Wah Press, Singapore
This book was printed on totally chlorine-free Nymolla Matte Art paper.
Production supervision by Stanley Redfern and Ginger Boyer
Designed by Kaelin Chappell